6TH GRADE

SUPERNATURAL

ABIGAIL'S CURSE

Cover art by Cristiana Voinea and ArtCorgi.com.

ISBN: 978-0-9906925-8-4

CHAPTER ONE

A lot of people are afraid of ghosts. But I don't mind them very much.

Most ghosts are harmless, friendly even.

It's the nasty ones you gotta look out for.

We live on Sparrow Hill in a house every kid I know thinks is haunted. Every chance I get I'm trying to find a way to assure them they're wrong.

Trouble is, they're not.

If I could convince any of the kids at school to come over, I would tell them that my little brother, Tyler, is the one who had drawn all over my bedroom walls. I would *not* say that the ghost of a five-year-old girl resides under my bed, and that she particularly enjoys my colored pencils. I would also tell them that the mess in the pantry is because my mother gets sloppy when she's cooking. I would *not* say that the ghoul who calls the little closet home is confused and, instead of trying to devour our flesh, keeps having a go at the cereal boxes.

But it doesn't need to go nearly that far, because no kid has ever had the courage to make it all the way up our front steps, much less inside.

It's definitely not my preference to be in a family of *parallels*. You know, ghost-seers. It would be a lot easier to make friends if I *couldn't* see what I can. And a lot easier to fit in in sixth grade if my parents would just move us into a normal house like everybody else.

I don't think Mom likes the situation much, either. Certainly not living on creepy old Sparrow Hill, at least. And on top of being stuck in the falling-down house passed down through Dad's family, she's the only one of us that *isn't* a Parallel. Tyler and I get the gift from Dad's side, so she's always the odd man out, as blind to the blood dripping down the walls as any other normal person.

Not that we have to stare at blood-dripping walls every day. Sometimes it's slime. Or ooze. Or green, boogery glop. Or, once, something that looked a lot like oatmeal.

But most days, I only see a couple *friendlies* flitting in and out of locked closets or pushing their vapor through classroom walls. And on the day that I met Abigail Stone, I had no reason to think that anything out of the ordinary was about to happen.

I flew down the front walk past Minnie, the girl ghost that hovers on our front lawn most mornings. She floated sullenly beside the mailbox, just like she did every day, silent and brooding. I caught her eye for a moment, and she opened her mouth like she was about to speak. Any other time I would have been thrilled to hear what it was she finally had to say after her years of silence, but we were late. I scrambled to make it through the folding door of the bus before it shut and I was stuck with a long walk to school. As we pulled away from the house, she raised up one hand in my direction. I waved back at her, hoping she'd still be feeling chatty after school.

On the bus, Jason Harris, the seventh grader who died three years ago after he tried jumping off the roof of his house into the backyard swimming pool (the idiot), talked my ear off as usual. Today he seemed convinced that he and his buddy, Tom, would be meeting up after school to make stink bombs. He tried to jostle me with his elbow as if I were in on the plan, conveniently ignoring the fact that a little spectral vapor couldn't move my solid body an inch. I shivered as the heat was sucked out of the blood in my arm where he had touched it, and wrapped my coat tighter around me.

Tyler rested his elbows on the seat back behind us.

"What are you gonna blow up?" he asked, his eyes wide and a little too hungry.

"You don't need to know how to blow anything up," I said, glaring back at him.

"What?" he said, a false look of hurt on his face. "I'm just learning about the world."

Most days I wished I could keep Tyler from learning anything at all. I had been a victim of one-too-many of his experiments. I no longer believed there was any value whatsoever left in scientific exploration.

"It'll be epic, Zan," Jason said. "Just meet me right here after school and I'll give you the instructions. Old Fitzsimmons'll never see it coming!"

Mr. Fitzsimmons was our school principal, and I was willing to bet that he could smell a stink bomb a mile away.

"No thanks," I said. "I'd rather not."

"Have it your way," he said, leaning back against the

seat and folding his arms.

"Oh, come on, Zander," Tyler complained, punching me in the arm.

"Ow!" I said. "You little creep."

The bus rolled to a stop, and we both stood up and wrestled our backpacks back on.

"Tell ya about it later, squirt!" Jason hooted after Tyler as we got off the bus.

And, sure enough, as I watched him crossing the street towards the elementary school, there was a bounce in his step that hadn't been there at breakfast. I sighed and made a mental note to stay far away from Tyler's bedroom that night.

So, like I said, the day was progressing in completely ordinary fashion. So much so that I didn't even see the *nasty* flitting between the sink drains in the boys bathroom until he slid fully out of one and slammed the back of my head into the wall tile.

"Ow!" I yelped, clutching the spot where my skull had knocked against the wall. I looked up and he glared at me, sickening yellow eyes glinting with malice.

What was a nasty doing *here?*

I was just pulling the amulet from around my neck when someone opened the door to the bathroom, and the nasty zoomed away, up through the ceiling.

Great.

I ignored the smirks of the boys who had come inside and pushed past them, rubbing my head as I walked down the hall. I searched the hallway, the unpleasant feeling of unexpectedly being thrust into danger swirling in my stomach. Most ghosts aren't evil, but Nasties are different. They delight in causing misery and pain, especially to Parallels. Too many Nasties in the same place at once could get downright dangerous, and luckily sightings were rare. I hadn't seen one in over a year. Wait until Dad heard.

But my search for the bathroom monster came up empty. The nasty had vanished.

Not for long, I thought.

I tucked the amulet back underneath my shirt and walked into class. I slumped into my desk, my mind buzzing. In my head I listed the different methods of attack I could use if it showed up again. The amulet, of course, would be easiest. I had one with me, for one thing, and nobody would understand what was going on if they saw me using it. Last time I had seen a nasty at school, I did away with it with one *ZAP,* and nobody had been the wiser. Dad had been thrilled when I told him that night over dinner, and I still felt a warm feeling of pride in my chest as I remembered. It had been my first solo banishing.

I could use an ousting broom, but the only one I knew of was sitting at home, propped up against our kitchen cabinets. Nasties were drawn to Parallels, and Mom got awfully cranky whenever they appeared in her otherwise spotless kitchen, throwing her tomatoes and dumping entire bags of cat food on the floor. Mom didn't have the sight, but over the years she had become a nasty-hunter in her own right. All I can say about that is, if you see an angry mother wielding a large broomstick, you'd better get out of the way quick, kid *or* nasty. Sometimes unexpected success can come from ordinary people if they put their mind to something.

One remaining option I had, only as a last resort, was my dad. Dad was always draped with an assortment of objects that were meant to do away with all sorts of undesired guests, dead or living. In the event that my amulet would fail, I knew he would have an alternate on hand that would do the job.

Gradually I became aware that the classroom had gone silent, and I looked up to see why, wondering if maybe Ms. Walker had asked me a question that I hadn't heard.

But that wasn't it. At the head of the class, Ms. Walker's hand placed tentatively on her shoulder, stood a girl I had never seen before. Ms. Walker looked down at her nervously, and then took her hand away as if worried the girl might chomp it off.

"Class," she said. "This is Abigail Stone. She's joining us all the way from California."

A collective gasp went up around the classroom. *California.* Land of beaches and movie stars and all things glitter.

I gasped, too. But not for the same reasons as everyone else. I had much better justification than the mention of sunshine to be sucking in my breath.

Because, clinging to the wall behind Abigail Stone, crouched over the doorway looking ready to pounce into her black, greasy hair, hung the biggest, slimiest nasty I had ever seen.

CHAPTER TWO

There were two.

He was different from the one in the bathroom; that one had been the size of a bulldog. Unpleasant, but manageable.

This one was more like a Great Dane, and it was staring at the students like it was getting ready to have a late breakfast.

Abigail Stone stood at the head of the class, grimacing around as if daring anyone to introduce themselves. I thought people from California were supposed to be nice looking. All that sun and sand and avocados. But Abigail was skinny and pale, her jet black hair framing her gray, bitter face. Well, little did she know that she was about to become that nasty's first course.

I stood up from my desk, knocking my chair over behind me as I did so. Scattered chuckles erupted around the classroom. Much more bravely than I felt, I held the amulet up to my eye.

The nasty didn't even see it coming. But Abigail did. Her eyes grew wide as golf balls as I squared off against the hovering creature.

"No!" she shouted, her superior pretense forgotten.

But she was too late. A purple stream of power, invisible to the rest of the class, burst from the amulet, hitting the nasty square in the chest. His sickening yellow eyes bugged, and he vanished backwards through the wall above the door. A gentle rain of dust falling to the classroom floor was all that remained of him.

"You idiot!" she said, glaring at me and stomping her foot (which I thought was a little childish, considering I had just saved her life). Then, hoisting up her backpack, she raced from the room, leaving Ms. Walker, and me, in a state of shock

"What on Earth is going on here?" Ms. Walker asked, turning her glare on me.

"Looks like DefenZander has done it again," snorted Miles Walsh from the back of the classroom.

On a regular day, I would have shot him a look and sat back down. But I was so distracted by Abigail's behavior that I could barely move. Of any of the reactions I might have expected from her, this one was definitely not on the list. Surprise, sure. Laughter, maybe. Or even the same sort of taunting as everyone else at Plainsbury Middle.

But anger?

I grabbed my backpack and took off after her.

"Mr. Casey!" said Ms. Walker.

I ignored her and burst through the doorway after Abigail. But once I was out of the classroom, I immediately wished I had stayed put. In the hallway, Abigail was nowhere to be found.

And the nasties were *everywhere*.

Hanging from the light fixtures. Throwing garbage at each other from the trash cans. Opening and slamming the lockers. One of them flew through the air clutching the corner of a school poster. *Fall Harvest Dance, Friday, September 20thth, 7:00,* the sign read. The nasty spun in a circle and the poster wrapped around his middle as he twirled. His eyes bugged as he realized he was caught in his own paper cocoon, and he slammed to the ground.

Nasties are so, well, nasty because they have a greater ability to use their bodies than your average ghost. Maybe they've been dead the longest. Or maybe they're just so angry that they can focus their energy better than a friendly. Either way, you want to be quick on your feet when you come face to face with one. Their aim is deadly accurate, and the last thing anyone needs is a fistful of dog poo hurled at their head.

I tried to catch the heavy classroom door behind me before it slammed into the frame. Too late. Twenty sets of eyes turned in my direction at the sound. I gulped.

They stared.

The first piece of garbage hit the side of my head with a *smack*. Wild, wicked laughter followed. The nasties chortled and congratulated each other on their clever insult.

Was that it? They were going to throw garbage? I stepped on the crumpled paper bag at my feet and shoved it away with my foot, gritting my teeth.

This was a mistake.

Their eyes darted back and forth between the bag on the floor and my face.

All at once, yesterday's sandwiches began raining down upon me. The laughter from the creatures mixed with their growling, grunting breath as they danced and guffawed at my humiliation. It was if I had interrupted some sort of celebration, and now I was the main entertainment. A sickening combination of old tuna fish and peanut butter crusts pervaded my nostrils as the onslaught continued.

I grappled for the amulet, half blinded when a smashed packet of ketchup struck near my eye. The casing dropped to the floor, but the contents still clung to one eyebrow, turning everything in my vision a bloody red as it dripped down to my cheek.

Finally, my fingers found the stone around my neck, and I held it up to my good eye. I went for the biggest nasty first, fixing him in my gaze through the clear, purple gem.

ZAP!

He went up in a cloud of smoke with a loud *POP*, nothing left of him but dusty bits floating down to the floor like an early snow.

All the nasties stopped, shocked by the sudden departure of their comrade. For the briefest moment, the hallway was silenced as they gaped at the empty space he had floated within just a moment before.

I took the opportunity to get another one in my

sights.

ZAP!

When they turned back to me, all the fun had drained from their eyes. Their smiles slipped away as if their faces had been greased. Maybe it had been a game to them at first. Not anymore. Then, with a rush, they all came for me at once.

I suddenly became aware that I was greatly outnumbered. I cursed the slamming of the door, wishing I had been able to sneak past them instead of attacking. That I had found a phone and called for help.

But it was too late now.

ZAP! ZAP!

They floated all around me, closing in, trapping me inside the slimy wall they made with their bodies.

I tried to push past them, but found them impossibly, impenetrably solid.

One of them opened his mouth wide, exposing his mossy, jagged teeth with a sadistic grin. My hands shook as I tried to focus the amulet on him. He held up a long, knobbed finger, waving it in my face, shaking his head back and forth.

"No, no, no," he snickered in a singsong voice.

The amulet fell through my sweaty fingers.

Every tiny hair on my skin stood straight up with terror. I hoped there was something left of me to find, something for my parents to bury, when this was over.

From nowhere, a cold, wet hand smacked me across the face. The blow stung, and the slime from the brute's fingers found its way into my ketchuped eye, quickly swelling it and sealing it shut.

Then, one of them grabbed the back of my shirt, and I realized I was airborne. My back hit the lockers on the opposite wall, deflating the air in my chest like a burst balloon. I slid down to the floor, gasping.

I couldn't move. I couldn't think. Their faces, snarling and fierce, seemed to crowd my brain, blocking out every other thought I had ever had. They were it, the last things I would see before I died. The tiny part of me, the part that still thought and plotted and fought, felt sorry. Sorry that my last vision alive hadn't been of something nice, something friendly. Like flowers or ice cream or the excited face of Aiden Wilcox's Husky puppy staring at me through the slats in our backyard fence.

The nasties stood over me, their bony chests moving up and down as they panted. Then, they started to part. I tried to back up further into the wall of lockers, but there was nowhere for me to go. Did they have some other weapon I hadn't seen? Surely they were planning to use it on me now. Well, let it be fast then, I thought. Let's get this over with.

But it wasn't a weapon that emerged from between the horde of nasties.

It was Abigail.

She stood over me, her arms folded across her chest, a satisfied smirk on her face. Over her left shoulder, a squat little nasty perched in midair, baring his tiny set of fangs at me like I was his morning snack. I struggled to make sense of what I was seeing. She gave it a wry glance.

"Who are you?" I croaked.

But she didn't answer. Instead, she began to turn away. She was going to leave me here with them, let them finish me off.

Then, echoing through the hallway, I heard the sweetest sound I could have imagined in a million years.

"What the devil is going on in here?"

It was the principal, Mr. Fitzsimmons, come to save the day.

CHAPTER THREE

We sat on opposite sides of the long, wooden bench.

Waiting.

The nasties had vanished as soon as Mr. Fitzsimmons had come into the hall, fleeing the scene like dust bunnies sucked into a vacuum cleaner. To him, it must have looked like Abigail and I had made all the mess, like it had been some sort of game for us to trash the school.

He couldn't have been more wrong.

I may have been just a kid, but I was old enough to know that it's the job, the *duty*, of a parallel to protect the living. Not only were we responsible for keeping people safe from the dark spirits of the underworld, we had to make sure they stayed clueless about the whole ghosts-flying-around situation.

And Abigail had made that task virtually impossible with her arrival.

Not to mention the fact that she had actually goaded the nasties into attacking me.

Why?

I gritted my teeth and stole a look at her. Her black, worn sweater wrapped around her middle like a straightjacket, contrasting with her pale, gray face. I noticed, with both satisfaction and disgust, that a large red zit was forming on the side of her greasy nose. The heel of her shoe tapped the floor impatiently. She glared into space as though this whole thing was my fault.

"I can't believe it," I breathed, just loud enough for the two of us to hear. "I can't believe you're a parallel and you sided with them. Wait until my dad finds out."

Her eyes flicked in my direction, but her face stayed set in a scowl.

"Great first day," I continued. "Nice of you to show up here and wreck everything."

She turned her chin away from me, facing the large window on the other side of the office. Her foot-tapping quickened and I sat back, satisfied that my words had an effect.

"Good thing you'll be out of here now," I went on, relentless. I had caught my breath again, but my head still throbbed. My eye was still stuck shut, a pulsing heat shooting through it into my head. The ketchup had dried now in my eyebrow, and the tightness on my skin beneath it irritated. "By tomorrow you'll be packing your bags back to California."

"Shut up!" she boomed suddenly, jumping to her feet.

Above our heads, several nasties poked their noses through the ceiling tiles, checking to see if it was time yet for another row. I automatically fumbled for the amulet.

The door behind us opened at that moment, and Mr. Fitzsimmons stepped out into the waiting area.

"Inside, please," he said. "Both of you."

We rose from the bench and slunk through the open office door. I wondered what sort of punishment was about to be laid on both our heads for Abigail's crimes. Mr. Fitzsimmons indicated the two chairs across from his desk and closed the door behind us. Then, stuffing the untucked flap of his shirt back into his pants over his round stomach, waddled back over to sit before us.

"You are both suspended for the rest of the day," he

began.

"But you don't understand—" I started.

"I understand more than you do, Mr. Casey," he said over me. "The mess you both made in the hallways of this school was disgraceful. I don't know what has gotten into you, but in addition to your suspension you will serve in detention for one week every day after school when you return."

"Mr. Fitzsimmons," I started again, trying to look more rational, more adult. He wasn't having it.

"I will accept no argument," he said shortly. He sat heavily into his chair, his shirt immediately becoming untucked again. "Mr. Jones is out there cleaning up your handiwork now, and I've a right mind to make you both help. Unfortunately, that is something the district will not allow. As such, I have instead called your parents to come retrieve you, and they should be arriving shortly. Go now, both of you."

That was it; my chance of escaping this disaster unscathed was lost. He had already called our parents. Mom was going to kill me.

Abigail stood from her seat and made for the door.

"One more thing, Ms. Stone," Mr. Fitzsimmons said. "Here at Plainsbury Middle School, we expect better of our students than that which you displayed this morning. Indeed, you are suspended on your very first day at this school. I hope that you will consider your behavior more carefully upon your return. That is all."

He opened a large beige folder from a stack on his desk and turned his attention to whatever was inside.

Probably our records, I thought. *No kid can trash a whole school corridor and expect to get away with it not being written in our files. In ink.*

Great.

I turned to follow Abigail out of the room, but she was already gone and walking through the double doors that led to the parking lot.

I turned back to Mr. Fitzsimmons, considered arguing one last time. But my curiosity got the better of me, and I raced after Abigail instead.

By the time I reached her, she was already striding down the long lawn towards the curb.

"Hey!" I shouted behind her. She didn't stop, didn't even seem to hear me. I sped up. "Hey!" I called again, angry at her dismissal. I wasn't done with her yet.

I reached her and grabbed her shoulder, spinning her around to face me. But then my words caught in my throat, and I stood staring at her, lost for words.

21

Because she was crying.

I looked around for a minute, unsure of what to do. Usually, in the life of an eleven-year-old, there's always some adult mulling around, someone responsible that a kid can count on to deal with things like skinned knees and broken arms and crying girls. But she and I stood alone on the grass, no help in sight.

Not to be dissuaded, I pushed on.

"Look, I don't know what you think you're doing here, but nasties aren't allowed to just go flying through the hallways. We have rules."

She folded her arms over her chest, her eyes on the ground.

"You hurt them," she said quietly. "When you used your stone. You can't do that."

"Can't do that?" I asked, incredulous. "I'm sorry, but when I see a slimy monster hovering over someone's head, even *your* head, I'm going to do something about it. And you, you just stood there and let them attack me, didn't you? They would've killed me if it weren't for Mr. Fitzsimmons coming in."

"They wouldn't have killed you. And anyways, what did you expect them to do?" she asked, her temper rising through her tears. Her hands flew to her hips. "Wouldn't

22

you fight back if you were attacked?"

"Yeah, but it's not—"

"What?" she sneered. "It's not the same? It *is* the same, and you know it." She angrily brushed away a trickle of snot, unable to contain it on top of the tears. Disgusting. "Maybe next time you should think about who you're aiming that thing at before you go blasting people out of the air."

"They're not *people*," I yelled back at her. "They're horrible and vicious and, well, *nasty*."

"They're my friends," she choked.

We stood face to face, staring daggers at each other. In the street, the soft sound of tires rolling over asphalt distracted me, and I looked over.

A large, pink minivan had parked in the red zone in front of the school. A tidy, brown-haired woman rolled down the passenger window and called out.

"Abigail!"

I looked back and forth between the bubble gum car and Abigail's wide, horrified eyes.

"Is that your *mom*?" I asked.

"Shut up!" she said again, and she picked up her backpack and ran to the van, slamming the door behind her.

CHAPTER FOUR

I sat in the grass for over an hour, but it wasn't too long before I realized Mom wasn't going to bother picking me up. Which meant I was in trouble.

Big trouble.

Behind me the bell rang for lunch, and I heard the happy chatter of the other kids on their way out into the yard, freed from their classrooms for a short reprieve at last. When the smell of cafeteria pizza drifted down to my nostrils, both disgusting and tantalizing, I finally got up to start the trek home.

I just didn't get it. Why had so many nasties suddenly emerged with the arrival of Abigail? And she seemed to think they were friendly.

No, not friendly. Her friends.

I wondered how things had been for her at her other school. Surely if she had had the nasties following her around there, too, there would have been signs. Other people, even if they couldn't see the monsters, would have witnessed the destruction they left in their wake.

I raised my hand to the back of my head, absently rubbing the spot where it had hit the bathroom wall earlier.

It just didn't make any sense. How had she befriended them? And why?

Half an hour later I rounded the last turn on Huckleberry Trail and started the long climb up the Sparrow Hill towards my house. One thing I knew for certain was that an absolute wave of nasties had accompanied Abigail when she moved to Plainsbury. And that could only mean one thing.

Somewhere, somehow, a gateway had been opened.

Suddenly, the seriousness of the situation dawned on me. If that doorway could let through a dozen or more nasties, what else might be waiting on the other side for an opportunity to slip past?

I broke into a run as our front door came into view, barreling up the walkway towards the one person who might be able to help.

As I pushed through the front gate, Minnie floated, her face hopeful, at the step. She raised one arm towards me as I flew by, as if she meant to catch my hand. But I was focused like a laser beam on my destination.

"Sorry, Minnie!" I called over my shoulder. "We'll have to talk later!"

I reached out for the doorknob and found it ice cold. I opened the door to find the house butler, Edgar, standing at attention. He had clearly been trying to open the door for me, but had only succeeded in freezing the handle, unable to move a solid object so large. Edgar had tended this house for hundreds of years, having died abruptly after testing his master's dinner for poison.

Little known fact: Most houses have a dead butler tending the front door, even the new, cookie cutter-type houses. This is because so many of them have died working for the families they so faithfully served. It's really too bad, and as a group they're definitely underpaid, considering the risk. I often think I'd like to have a real butler someday. I mean, Edgar can be downright helpful sometimes. But then I remember the likelihood that a live butler would die a horrible death, and I try to forget the whole idea.

"Thanks, Edgar," I huffed, and headed for the attic.

"Zander!" called Mom from somewhere out of sight, her tone icy.

I ignored her and heaved open the door that led to Dad's study, taking the stairs two at a time.

"Dad!" I called, breathless. The air up here was dusty and thick, as though no one had been in to clean in a hundred years. Dad rarely let anyone up into his study, and people bearing feather dusters were no exception. "Dad?" I called again.

I heard a shuffling noise from the far end of the room and turned to find the wobbly figure of my father trying to climb out from a sort of cave he had created for himself. As he attempted to straddle over two enormous stacks of books piled on the floor, he lost his balance, tumbling to the ground with a crash.

"Zander!" my mom yelled from the bottom of the stairs.

"Dad, I need to talk to you," I said, panting.

He looked up from the mess, his eyeglasses hanging precariously over his face by one ear.

"What?" he sputtered.

"Dad, it's about the nasties," I said. "It's important."

"Nasties?" he asked, his face automatically alarmed.

"ZANDER!" Mom's footsteps were pounding up the

stairs now. We both turned.

He launched from the pile of books and headed her off at the door. I headed deeper into the room to hide.

We all knew that Mom tolerated Dad's obsession with the paranormal, but her patience only went so far. He blocked her path at the top of the stairs, and I saw the tip of her nose stick out over his shoulder, peering around into the room. I slunk back against the wall, just out of her sight.

"Where is he, Robert?" she demanded.

"What?" he said. "Who?"

"Don't you play dumb with me, my *darling*." She was pushing him now, trying to disrupt his balance so she could make her way past. "Let me by, you old fool."

"I'm working up here at present," he said matter-of-factly. "I cannot be disturbed."

"Hogwash," she said. "Zander, I know you're in there!" She had stopped trying to knock Dad down, and settled for yelling into the room, knowing I could hear. "And when you come out you're gonna get a reckoning like you've never had before. Do you understand me? I couldn't *believe* it when I got the call—"

"Yes, yes, Dear" Dad said, forcing her backwards down a couple of steps.

"Don't you push me," Mom said angrily. I could hear her stumbling on the stairs. "*You'll* be dealing with me, too. Keep an eye on your chocolate pudding tonight, *Dear*."

It was an idle threat, but Dad took everything to do with sweets almost as seriously as threats from the underworld.

Mom's footsteps echoed down the narrow staircase.

"Now, Darling," Dad sputtered, suddenly alarmed at the risk to his dessert. He waved a finger after her and started down the steps. "Don't you go playing around with my pudding. You know that I look forward to my sweets all day long and—"

The door at the bottom of the staircase slammed, and his thought was left unspoken, hanging in the musty air.

"*Dad*," I hissed. "This is more important than chocolate."

He came around the corner again, and I could see the cost of his support mirrored in his sad eyes. I sighed.

"I'll give you some of my pudding, ok?" I said.

"Don't kid yourself, Zander," he said hopelessly, walking across the room and slumping into a chair. "She's just going to ruin yours, too."

He looked as if there had been a death in the family.

"Dad, there were nasties at school today," I said.

He perked up, the loss of sweets instantly, though temporarily, forgotten.

"What?" he asked. "What happened?"

I told him the story of Abigail. How she had come from out of town. How the nasties had been drawn to her, and that she seemed to like their presence. The more I spoke, the wider his eyes became.

"That was the weirdest part," I went on. "She got really upset when I tried to banish them. She said they were her friends."

"You banished them, did you? You used the amulet?"

"Yeah, but there were too many," I said. "They attacked me, Dad, all at once."

"How many?" he asked.

"At least ten, maybe more," I said.

He let out his breath in a long, low whistle.

"What?" I asked.

"She's a *medium*," he breathed.

"What? What's that?"

"Not so different from us, but I'm afraid her powers are much more dangerous. Mediums, if left untrained, open doorways into the other realms. She must not understand. Though how she could get to be your age and still not—"

He jumped up suddenly, a frenzied look on his face.

"We have to go."

"What?" I said. "Where are we going?"

"We have to find this friend of yours," he said. "What was her name? Alice?"

"Abigail," I said. "And she's not my friend."

He wrenched open the door and started down the stairs. He must have lost his balance, because before I could catch up with him, a loud, tumbling crash filtered up through the old drywall. I ran to the doorway and looked down. At the bottom of the long staircase, he lay in a heap like a pile of dirty laundry.

"Are you okay?" I asked, jumping down the stairs after him.

"Serve you right!" I heard my mom yell from the other side of the house.

But he was already struggling to get to his feet.

"I'm okay," he called, and then more loudly, "I'm okay, Darling! No need to worry!"

There was no response.

"How are we going to find her?" I asked. "We don't know where she lives."

"Oh, don't you worry," he said. "When nasties come together out of the void, there's always a trail."

CHAPTER FIVE

Five minutes later we were barreling down the hill in Mom's old minivan. It was a hand-me-down she had forced on Dad when the engine light kept coming on last summer. It was to be his job to repair it before taking it for his own, which, of course, he never did. The dashboard squeaked and the engine groaned as we dodged the potholes in the road from our house, bouncing down the hill like a warped rubber ball.

Dad pulled out a pair of battered glasses and shoved them onto his face over the glasses he already wore. He looked completely insane. Immediately, his gaze shifted towards the sky, and his jaw dropped open.

"There," he breathed, pointing into the blank twilight. "There it is. Oh, wow." He shuddered. "I've never seen anything like *this* before. Here, look."

He ripped the second pair of glasses from his nose and thrust them at me. Tentatively, I held them up.

And immediately stopped breathing.

A sickly green trail of light was hovering right above our car, like an aurora gone terribly wrong. I shrunk back into my seat. Long fingers of acid haze fanned out across the night like a spider with a hundred legs, all meeting together in a bright, burning glow at the edge of town.

"Give them to me," he said.

I couldn't move, could barely understand his words.

His fingers fumbled across my shocked face and wrenched the glasses off, shoving them unceremoniously back onto his own. With their removal, the green instantly vanished. It seemed, though, that the sight was burned into my brain, and my eyes darted around, searching for some other sign of the threat.

"What was that?" I finally asked when my voice returned.

"Not was," he said. "*Is.* It's a specter trail. Your little friend is going to let in all the ghosts from Bishop County if we don't get to her soon."

I shivered as I imagined what a hundred, a thousand nasties could do if they were set loose on the town. We'd be outnumbered. We'd be toast.

"But I don't understand," I said. "How is this happening?"

He sighed heavily as he turned the car, screeching, onto East Boulevard.

"I don't know for sure," he said. "It's not the same thing as one or two nasties breaking through, like you've seen in the past, when they slip through a crack in the gate. Or," he grimaced, "when some old fool opens it for a quick second to let a few through."

He was thinking of Gramps. It had been the old man's idea of a joke, but nobody had thought it was funny except him. Two years ago on Halloween, Gramps concocted a plan to send Dad into a tizzy with a few unexpected trick-or-treaters. Somehow, he had managed to let just three of the nasties into our world, but that had been enough to trash the house. Even Tyler had run for it, hiding under his bed for hours after we had managed to banish them. That had been the year I learned how to use my amulet. It had also been the year Mom threatened to kick Gramps out of the house for good. Lots of Mom's threats weren't real; they were just her way of blowing off steam. But the snarl carved into her face that night hadn't quickly been forgotten, not by any of us, and Gramps hadn't so much as cracked a joke at her expense since.

"But this is different," Dad went on. "Somewhere, and from the looks of it, right there at the center of the trail, a gate has been thrown wide."

Gateways were what we called the entrances to and from the underworld. In order for humans to live a happy, peaceful life, all gates needed to remain closed. But sometimes, by accident or prank or just the collected will of a horde of nasties, they would burst open. And when that happened you could forget watching Saturday morning cartoons. All bets were off.

I searched again for the trail, but without the glasses, all I saw was the first stars popping out into the sky.

It didn't take long for us to reach the place. Dad pulled up in front of the house and jumped out of the car, staring up into the sky at the sight only he could see. In the driveway, the pink minivan was neatly parked, and as we passed it on our way to the front door, Dad stopped walking, distracted.

"Nice ride," he said to himself, admiring the clean lines of the brand new van, so cherry compared to his old, beat up junker. He ran his hand along the edge of the smooth, immaculate paint, not yet dented by parking lot mishaps or splattered with the poop of birds passing by overhead. "Oh, yeah," he went on, "I need to get me one of these."

"Dad," I said, irritated. "Don't we have more important things to worry about right now?"

"What?" he said, looking up through the fog of his daydream. "Oh! Yes! Quite right."

I jogged up the front steps and crammed my palm against the doorbell. He shuffled up to stand beside me, his attention grudgingly torn from admiring the van. I saw him steal a glance back over his shoulder at it as we waited.

The door opened, and the same, tidy woman I had seen that afternoon stood before us. She smiled, but behind the smile, her eyes were hard.

"Well, hello," she said. "Who might you be?"

"Hi," I said, a little unsure. I looked at Dad, whose eyes were still glued to the van. "I'm Zander. I'm in class with Abigail."

Her eyes narrowed and the fake smile dropped.

"Yes," she said, her tone sharp. "I've heard about you. You're the boy who caused all the commotion today, then, are you?"

"What?" I said. "No, it wasn't *me*." I jabbed Dad in

the side with my elbow, and he turned to face Abigail's mom.

"Hmm?" he asked, distracted. "Oh, yes. What a glorious vehicle you have there," was all he thought to say.

"*Dad*," I snarled.

"What?" he sputtered. "Oh, of course. Might we have a word with, ah, Annabelle, is it?"

"Abigail," I corrected.

"Yes, that's right," he said.

"And why, might I ask, do you want to speak with her?" she asked. "Haven't you caused enough—"

"It's okay, Mom," came Abigail's voice from inside. She poked her head out and stepped into view. She smiled pleasantly at her mother. "I can handle him."

Both Dad and I gasped and took a step back. A nasty was hovering right over Abigail's shoulder, the same one I had seen in the hallway, bobbing up and down like an apple in a tub.

"I think not," said Abigail's mom. "You know how I hate interruptions during the dinner hour. And you're in quite a lot of trouble already, young lady."

"*Mom,*" she said. "Just give me a minute to talk to them. Okay? It won't take long."

Her mother looked back and forth between us and her daughter, and was just opening her mouth to argue again when a buzzer sounded from somewhere inside the house. She huffed.

"You've got two minutes," she said, slamming her hands onto her hips. "Do you hear me?" She turned and stormed off towards the sound, and Abigail stepped outside and shut the door.

"What do you want?" she asked stiffly, her friendly demeanor evaporating. She crossed her arms over her chest and glared at us.

"Well, my dear," Dad began.

"You've opened a portal and let in all these nasties and now they're going to overrun the town and destroy everything!" I blurted.

Abigail's eyes widened.

"What?" she said. "No, I didn't."

"I'm afraid you did," Dad said. "There is no other explanation, and all paths lead here to this house." He looked up at the sky again, his face both worried and excited, like a little kid watching a fireworks show for the first time.

"I didn't open anything," she said. "There's just more flyers here than where I came from, that's all."

"Flyers?" I asked. "You mean nasties?"

"Why would you call them nasties?" she asked, turning to face the one floating next to her left ear. "They're so sweet." She tickled it under its chin and it did a sort of flip in midair, clearly pleased. Then it turned to us and blew a loud raspberry, spraying us with a fine mist of goo.

"Ugh," I said, wiping my face with my sleeve. "Well, whatever you think of them, we need to close the gateway before something terrible happens."

"It's true," Dad said. "It's only a matter of time before something bigger breaks through. Such an event could cause irreparable damage to our town, to our world. Nobody knows what would happen if the doorway were to remain open as it is now. It could be the end of all humanity."

Abigail glared, a mean smirk spreading across her face.

"Oh, I don't believe that," she said smoothly. "Besides, it seems to me this place could use a little livening up." She turned away and gripped the doorknob.

"Wait," I said. "Don't you want to make friends here? *Real* friends?"

Her face fell.

"You can't do that if every kid in school is going to end up attacked by all the nasties you're letting in."

Her face hardened again, and she smirked.

"I *do* have real friends," she said. "They're just not alive anymore. Anyways, I'm not interested in being friends with kids when I have an endless supply of much more interesting options. Kids are mean and spiteful, anyways."

"Like you, you mean?" I spat.

Her sneer faltered.

She opened the door behind her and stepped inside, slamming it in my face without another word.

Dad and I exchanged a glance.

"Well," he finally said, removing the glasses, "that could have gone better."

I sighed.

That night we walked most of the way home. Mom's old minivan finally gave out just a few blocks from Abigail's house, sputtering to a slow, painful death on the side of the road. As we walked up the path towards our front door an hour later, I remembered I had meant to stop to talk to Minnie. But now, at this hour, she was nowhere to be found.

Oh, well. Tomorrow.

Our dinner sat plated on the counter, stone cold. The house was dark and quiet except for the light snore coming from the ghoul in the pantry. Dad placed our plates into the oven to warm and, searching through the fridge, found two fancy cups filled with the coveted chocolate pudding. He retrieved a spoon and took a hopeful bite, then grimaced.

"Ugh!" he said, running to the sink to spit it out. "I told you." He cupped some water into his hand and washed out his mouth.

"What?" I asked. "What's wrong with it?"

He turned and leaned against the counter, wiping his face regretfully with a dish towel.

"It seems, my son, that your mother, ah, *accidentally* used salt in our dessert instead of sugar. I must remind her to check the labels more carefully when she's cooking."

I stared down at my pudding, heart in my stomach. Then I pushed back from the counter.

"I'm going to bed," I said.

"Yes, I expect that's wise," he said. He looked tired, the manic light in his eyes having been extinguished by the one final insult of the evening. "Come to my study in the morning. We'll figure out what to do."

CHAPTER SIX

Dad's eyes were tired and droopy as he looked at me over his morning coffee. We were back in his study where, apparently, he had spent most of the night trying to figure out what we should do next.

"It would be one thing if we had reinforcements," he said, staring hopelessly into his mug. "But it's just our family around these parts, and, let's face it, only you and I would be much use in this situation."

He was right. Gramps would probably think the whole event was some sort of joke. Tyler, while theoretically old enough to help us, was the type of kid to go looking for trouble, not banish it. Mom, on the other hand, if she had had the gift, would have made an excellent nasty-hunter. She was already terrifying to us who were still living. But somehow I doubted she would be much use with nothing but the banishing broom to use. And a woman running around town waving a broom in the air would cause too much talk. Without the sight, she could do nothing to help. I didn't even know if a normal person could learn how to use an amulet at all.

We sat across from each other, both of us thinking the same thing.

We needed a team. Some sort of nasty-fighting task force. But who?

"The best we can do, for now, is for you to talk to this Arielle—"

"Abigail."

"Yes, that's right. For you to talk to her and make her see reason. And *be nice.* She's not going to hear you out if you're snarking at her about yesterday. You'll have the whole day at school with her today. She can't run away from you there."

"I'll have detention with her, too," I said, trying to imagine how I might be able to corner her in the dungeon of a classroom where detention was held. I had only seen the room from afar, the heavy metal door mercilessly closing as the villains of the day were trapped inside, punished for their deeds with unbearable, silent boredom. I shuddered.

"Yes," Dad said, getting to his feet. "That's the best we can do, for now. I'll circle around the area in case anything goes wrong. I won't be far."

"What about your work here?" I asked.

"Zander," he smiled, "this may be a terrifying event for us. But the truth is we are on the brink of discovery here. Already we've seen more fascinating phenomena in the past twenty four hours than most parallels do in their entire lifetimes. I just hope we survive it."

As I rode the bus to school, I didn't care or even notice whatever forbidden information Jason Harris was passing along to Tyler. Absently, I told myself to expect the smell of rotten eggs from somewhere inside the school later in the day.

I didn't care about eggs or math class or anything, though. All I cared about was finding Abigail, and then sticking to her like glue until she was willing to hear me out.

The hallway was now spotless, the sign for the dance hastily taped back together and re-hung on the wall. I walked cautiously towards first period, the amulet ready and clenched in my fist, on the lookout for any trouble.

Floating dreamily past, the pretty lady who had died from eating tainted Mexican hot sauce tilted her head in my direction in greeting. I tried to smile back, but all I managed was a sort of painful smirk.

Dad told me once she had been the librarian here when he was a kid, and that her death had sent a panic through the town. Botulism. That was the stuff that had killed her. It had grown like wildfire on the rim of the jar at the restaurant, then grew like wildfire in her belly, paralyzing her to an untimely death. I had read an article about it because I have a sort of phobia about not being able to use my arms and legs. When you've had enough ghosts accidentally bump into you and make your limbs go numb, you think about these things.

Now, I realized, concern about the freshness of restaurant condiments was the least of my worries.

But despite my searching, the torrent of nasties from the day before were nowhere to be seen. It wasn't until Abigail entered the classroom, just one minute before the bell, that I caught a glimpse of the little one that bobbed ceaselessly over her shoulder. I grimaced at it, disgusted by its gray, seeping skin and bugging eyeballs. It was almost like some kind of pet. But where most other girls might like to smuggle something cute and fuzzy into class to keep them company, this companion was downright disgusting.

Abigail saw me looking at her little beast, and glared. Then, turning on her heel, she swiftly made her way to the back of the room and sat down.

Ms. Walker, seeing the exchange between us, cleared her throat loudly.

"Good morning, class," she said. "I expect that today we will not be experiencing the same…*disturbances* as yesterday. Would that be a fair assumption?" Her stare flitted back and forth between me and Abigail, and I nodded dutifully.

"Good," she said.

I turned to look at Abigail. She stared straight ahead as if I didn't even exist.

The morning passed slowly. At break, I realized Abigail and I might not have any more classes together. Yesterday we hadn't even made it through first period before catastrophe struck, and it was entirely possible that we wouldn't be seeing each other again until late in the day.

And I was proven right. She disappeared down the hallway towards math while I was forced to head the other way towards science. I watched her go, nose in the air as she strode away, while all the other kids shied away from her, clearing a path so they wouldn't be forced to get too close to this new, strange girl.

You couldn't blame them. They had only gotten a split-second glimpse of Abigail before she had taken off out of the classroom yesterday. And then what had happened? All they knew was that the corridor had been trashed, presumably by her.

And me.

But, while I was admittedly somewhat of an outcast myself, I still ranked one rung up from Abigail. After all, I had lived in Plainsbury my whole life. I could be trusted. At least enough to ask questions.

"What happened out there yesterday?" Brad Coleman asked during morning break. He had sauntered up to me like he owned the place and everyone in it. On a normal day, I might have taken the bait, eager to make friends with, or at least appease, someone so high up the social food chain. But not today. Instead, I was scanning the tops of the heads, searching for Abigail's snarling black mass of hair.

"Huh?" I asked, distracted.

"I said, what happened yesterday? You know, with the new freaky girl?" He crossed his arms over his chest

49

and puffed up, trying to make it appear that he had muscles underneath his t-shirt. Across the hall, his gang of followers stood waiting. And, I noticed, several other people in the hall had suddenly gone quiet as well, eager to hear my explanation. Only Brad had been brave enough to actually confront me about it, and now they all waited for me to spill a juicy piece of gossip, like dogs waiting for a chunk of fresh meat.

"She's not freaky," I said, automatically defending Abigail. I didn't like her much, but the truth was, she and I had some very important traits in common. It didn't seem right to join in bashing her. "She's just... different."

Snickers came from the boys.

"But how did it happen?" It was Candace McCarthy, timidly approaching us despite dozens of sets of eyes watching her every move. Candace and I were friendly. Not friends, exactly, but she didn't sneer at me like a lot of the other kids did. "I mean, this place was *trashed*," she went on. "Did you guys get into an argument?"

Suddenly, I felt backed into a corner. Everyone seemed very aware of whatever it was that was going on between me and Abigail. Too aware. And, as I well knew, too many questions about odd occurrences around school never led anywhere good.

So I lied.

"Um, well, Abigail was just upset with me because I, uh, hurt her feelings."

"Hurt her feelings?" Brad asked. "By what, showing her your pretty necklace?"

Several people chuckled, but Candace's face stayed deadly serious.

"But how could you have hurt her feelings?" she asked. "You had just met her."

I felt like a cornered animal in a room with no exit. I needed to get out of here.

"Yeah, well, uh, it's complicated," I said, looking around for an escape. "The truth is, Abigail and I have met before." I hoped the story was convincing. "And we've never gotten along. You know what? I forgot my notebook back in Walker's class. See you guys." I took off down the hall back towards homeroom.

So much for my morning break.

I slammed the door behind me and leaned up against it, breathing hard. How on Earth was I supposed to explain what was going on to a group of sixth graders without freaking everybody out? And they weren't idiots, either, even if I preferred to think of them that

51

way. I was going to have my work cut out for me.

I walked over to the window and looked outside, immediately spotting Dad. He hadn't been kidding about not being far; I could have hit him in the head with a spit wad from here if I had wanted to. He was pacing around the front of the school, occasionally smashing the viewing glasses onto his face and staring up into the sky. Each time he did this, he froze with his mouth wide. Then, shaking himself, he would rip the glasses off and continue his loop, staring down at his feet, deep in thought while he stood ready to defend us against the nasties inside.

I considered going out to talk to him, trying to get him to leave, or at least hide. But, I realized, he was the only support I had if another nasty attack went down. I needed him close. I hoped none of the other kids would notice him out there during their social studies daydreaming.

I didn't see Abigail again until the end of the day at three o'clock detention, where she was finally forced to be in the same room with me. She had been avoiding me all day, not even showing her face at lunch. But I really couldn't blame her for that. I, myself, spent most of my lunch break sitting in a bathroom stall in the upstairs boys' room, hiding out from the incessant questions from my suddenly curious classmates.

Abigail slunk into the room, trying to move to the back of the class, as she had in the morning, but Mr. Jones was having none of it.

"I want you where I can see ya," he said, wiping crumbs from his track suit.

Mr. Jones was our P. E. teacher and, in typical fashion, was as big as a house. Today must have been his turn to monitor detention, which was particularly unfortunate for us, as he had also been the one to clean the hallway yesterday.

Abigail rolled her eyes and grudgingly took a seat two rows over from mine.

"Now," Mr. Jones drawled. "We can do this the easy way, or the hard way. The easy way goes like this. You be quiet and do your homework and don't cause any trouble. That sound like something you can manage?"

"What's the hard way?" Abigail's question, I was sure, had been asked before. I shot her a look, which she ignored.

"The hard way is you don't do as your told and end up suspended again. Or," he rustled the bag of chips gripped in his pudgy fingers, "you get expelled. Now, I don't think expulsion is something a little lady like you wants to deal with. Am I right?"

Abigail scowled.

"Alright then," he said. He sat back in his chair and put his feet up on the desk, munching the last of the chips from the bag and slurping the crumbs from his fingertips.

I took out the binder from my backpack and flipped it open. I actually had a ton of work I needed to do, yesterday's and today's. But there was a zero percent chance I was going to be able to concentrate on anything other than figuring out how to get Abigail alone.

Twenty minutes in, I was still staring at a blank page when a light snore caught my attention. I looked up to find Mr. Jones leaning back in his chair, his mouth wide. I took the opportunity.

"Hey," I whispered.

She ignored me.

"Hey, you can't ignore me forever, you know."

"Can't I?" she asked, not taking her attention away from her work.

"We need to talk," I said.

"We already talked."

I sighed.

"Where did all the others go?" I asked.

"I have it under control, okay?" she snarled, finally looking up at me. "You haven't seen any flyers today, have you?"

I inclined my head towards the disgusting monster floating above her shoulder. It turned around and shook its little butt at me.

"I mean, other than Ralph," she corrected.

"You *named* it?" I asked.

Mr. Jones gave a loud snort from the front of the room.

"That's beside the point," she said, keeping her voice low and her eyes on him. "The others are gone. Now leave me alone."

"I can't leave you alone," I said, irritated. "Don't you get it? I'm trained to banish nasties. My whole family has been doing it for, like, a thousand years. Whatever it is you're up to is about to blow up in your face."

She rolled her eyes.

"Fine," she snapped.

Mr. Jones snorted himself awake. We both looked down at our work, careful to look as if not a word had been spoken. He looked stupidly around for a minute, then leaned fully back in his chair, asleep again in an instant.

Abigail was scribbling furiously on a sheet of notepaper. She silently folded it and passed it over to me.

I kept my eyes on Jones as I grabbed the note and hid it under the desk. Then, when I was sure I was in the clear, I unfolded it and read:

My house. 10 o'clock tonight. Come alone.

CHAPTER SEVEN

"Hey, wait up," I called.

Dad was walking so fast I could barely keep up. He was excited, mumbling to himself as he watched the sky through his spectacles.

"Unlike anything...gonna blow anytime... untrained...end of the world." The phrases came out of his mouth in a jumble, the only thing tying them together the frantic look on his face.

"I don't know," I said. I was starting to wonder if Abigail was right. Maybe she did have things under control...somehow. After all, the only nasty I had seen all day had been the one on her shoulder. *Ralph*, she had called it. And it had seemed to be restrained enough. "Maybe it won't be so bad."

He stopped, turning to face me.

"Not so bad?" he asked, unbelieving.

He removed the glasses from his face and handed them to me. I took them, and pressed them over my eyes, ready to be proven wrong, as always.

And I was. Immediately.

Last night, the tendrils of power emanating from Abigail's house had been floating gently on the breeze, almost beautiful in their eerie glow.

Tonight, however, things had changed. Red sparks were shooting in and out of the great green light that had settled over the place. It was like a Christmas light factory was in the process of exploding. What was going on down there?

I quickened my pace and stayed close to Dad, suddenly concerned and a little scared.

"What is it?" I asked, handing the glasses back to him.

"You keep them," he said, pushing them away. "Maybe show them to her."

I put the glasses back on, terrified and fascinated by what I saw.

"A gateway is open, alright," he said, huffing. "What I can't figure out is why. Why would she want to let in monsters from the underworld? Do you know?"

I shook my head. I didn't. I couldn't imagine why anyone would want to spend their time face to face with a bunch of nasties. Not unless they had a death wish.

When we got to Abigail's street, I stopped, holding Dad back.

"She said to come alone," I said. "You can't follow me."

He grimaced, looking worriedly towards the tidy suburban neighborhood.

"It's not safe," he finally said.

"It'll be okay," I said. "She's still alive. And her family."

Still, he resisted.

"Look, can you hide somewhere or something? If she sees you she's gonna freak."

He sighed.

"Fine," he said. "I'll be close by. But listen." He grabbed my shoulder as I turned to walk away. "Remember. The whole point is to get her to come over to our side. If she's letting them in on purpose, and you two don't patch things up..."

"Right, okay," I said.

"We need her to help us close the gate," he said.

"I know, I know," I said, irritated at both the reminder and the fact that I was now supposed to make friends with the girl who had set a hallway full of nasties on me.

I turned away and walked towards her house. Dad was going to go around behind the neighbor's houses, sneak through the backyards until he could find a place to keep watch.

As I approached the place, my heart started pounding in my chest. The red sparks were constant, but silent. I wondered what it all meant. When I found myself standing frozen at the foot of her front walk, I wrenched the glasses from my eyes and stuffed them into my pocket. No sense being scared out of my wits if I didn't have to be.

I walked up to the front door. The house was dark. They must go to be early in the Stone family, I thought. I stood staring at the fine wood knocker and suddenly wondered what I should do. Should I ring the bell? That seemed unwise. The last thing I wanted was that foul mother of hers coming to answer. What, then?

"Hey." The quietest of whispers caught my attention from a large shrub to the side of the front porch. I looked over to see two enormous eyes staring at me from between the leaves.

"Hi," I whispered back.

"Follow me," she said.

She snuck out from behind the bushes and quietly darted around the side of the house. I followed, trying hard not to make a sound, cringing every time my foot snapped a twig or crinkled a leaf.

Abigail led me to a side door in the house and quietly pushed it open. She beckoned for me to follow. As we both stood in the darkness, she closed the door with a quiet click. We were in the laundry room.

"We just need to get you upstairs," she whispered. "Then I can show you."

Once out in the hallway, I saw that there was a light still on, only it was at the very back of the house. The low hum of a television echoed through the hall, and I looked at her nervously. She nodded encouragingly and beckoned me to follow.

We snuck through the downstairs and quickly found the staircase, darting up the thick carpeting as fast as we could. In another five seconds, we were in her room.

I stared around in the darkness, fascinated. I had never been inside a girl's bedroom before, and part of me expected to discover something sinister there, something to prove what I had always suspected about girls my age. That they were wimps. Not to be trusted. That there was some sort of plot that they were all in on, a plot to torture boys into liking things like flowers and dolls. But nothing about Abigail's room indicated anything of the sort. Even in the darkness I could tell that the walls were stark white, not the disgusting pink I had expected.

I guess she doesn't take after her mom.

But I already knew that.

She walked to the center of the room and quietly called, "Ralph!"

Instantly, the little monster popped out from the smooth white ceiling. A thin trickle of drool hung from his pointed teeth, and he smiled broadly at her. Then, seeing me, he growled.

"It's okay, Ralph," she said, trying to calm him. "I invited him in."

Ralph dropped from the ceiling and circled around Abigail's head like a dog who had been waiting all day for its master to come home.

"How long has he been in here alone?" I asked.

"Just ten minutes or so," she said.

Ralph bobbed up and down like a little kid on Christmas morning. Abigail looked towards him and smiled.

I guess he was attached.

"Alright, that's enough," she said, and Ralph came to rest in his usual spot over her left shoulder.

The whole situation perplexed me. For a minute there, I had almost been thinking Ralph was sort of... *cute*.

But no, that wasn't it. It's wasn't possible for a nasty to be cute.

Abigail sat down on the edge of her bed. I looked around and found a desk chair.

"See?" she said. "Everything's fine here. Everything's under control. Ralph is the sweetest thing." She tilted her head towards him and nuzzled against his decaying flesh.

I tried hard not to gag.

"What happened to the other ones?" I asked. "Wait. Nevermind that. How did they even get out in the first place?"

Up until this moment Abigail had seemed completely in control. It was clear that her house was fine, her family was fine, and apparently this one tiny nasty wasn't causing anybody any trouble. Except maybe me. But at my question, she looked around the room, a distinctly worried look on her face.

"I don't really know where they came from," she admitted. She looked like she expected them to descend from the ceiling at any moment. "But they're gone now."

"How did you get rid of them?" I asked.

She shrugged. "I just asked them to go. And they listened."

I snorted sarcastically.

"It's true," she said, stiffening. "I've always had a way with flyers. We've moved around a lot before now, and I've met new friends in each place. Ralph here is the first one who's ever followed me. And you're the first person I've ever met who can see them, too."

"Wait. Doesn't anyone else in your family see them?" I asked.

"No," she said. She seemed a little sad. "Just me."

"But how is that even possible?" I asked. "Parallels always run in families. I don't even think it's possible for —"

"I'm adopted."

My jaw dropped and the words faded on my lips.

It took me a minute to recover. I sat motionless, trying to figure out what to say, but coming up with nothing. Then, finally, I forced myself back on track.

"But that could mean *anything*," I said. "You could be anything. Anyone."

She shrugged again.

"Yeah, I guess," she said. "I've never told anybody about flyers. Well, I tried once to tell my mom, but she totally freaked. I didn't make *that* mistake again." She looked down at her fingers, which were fiddling in her lap. "I mean, you've seen her."

Yes, I had.

"What about friends?" I asked. How could she have never told a soul about being a parallel? It seemed impossible.

"Don't have many friends," she said, focusing intently now on not looking at me.

I stared across at her through the moonlight coming in her bedroom window, and I realized just how desperate her situation was.

"You should come with me, back to my house," I said. Then, realizing that we were sitting in the dark, corrected, "Not tonight, obviously. But tomorrow. After school. There's so much we can teach you. Dad says you're a medium, and that if you don't get training you could end up doing a lot of damage."

Immediately her defenses returned. She glared, and

Ralph started hissing in my direction.

"I don't need you to *teach* me," she growled. "I know what I'm doing."

"No, you don't," I argued. "I can't even believe you've survived this long without a guide." Suddenly, I felt infinitely grateful that I lived in the family I did. My whole family tree was littered with parallels. Hundreds of years of experiences were shared generation after generation. I guess that meant I had an advantage.

But Abigail didn't see it that way.

"Whatever," she said. "I held my own fine in the hallway yesterday, didn't I? They did what I asked them to, didn't they?"

She was getting to her feet now, clearly angry. I stood up, trying to backtrack.

"You, if I recall, were the one on the floor," she went on. "Hopeless and stupid. Like a baby."

"I am not a baby," I said, stung.

"Well, for someone who's not a baby, you sure looked relieved when Mr. Fitzsimmons walked in."

"That's not being a baby, that's being smart." I folded my arms across my chest.

"What, now you're calling me stupid?" she shot.

"If the shoe fits," I said.

This wasn't going at all as planned.

She looked ready to hurl *her* shoes at me.

"You're just jealous," she said, "because I can get them to do what I want and you can't. That's all this is."

"That's crazy," I spat. "You haven't seen this place through these." I pulled out Dad's glasses from my pocket and held them up.

"And what are those supposed to be, supernatural goggles? Please."

If it had been humanly possible, I was certain steam would have been pouring from my ears.

"You only say that because you haven't seen," I said. "So you don't—"

Suddenly, the floor shook beneath our feet. We both looked around the room, searching for the source of the disturbance. Ralph was bobbing up and down again. But this time he looked anxious.

"You need to leave," Abigail said, hands on her hips.

"What? Why?"

"Because you've upset me," she said. Then, pointing to the ceiling, "And *they* know about it."

They?

I looked up at the ceiling again, which was now sort of rolling, like a pot of boiling water in slow motion.

"Shall I just call them back, then?" she asked.

I stared at her, shocked.

She wouldn't.

But something about her snarl made me think she just might.

"Look," I started, trying to rally one last time. "We can help each other. We want the gate to be closed. You want to learn—"

"The only think I want," she said, "is you out of my bedroom. Now go."

My heart sank into my stomach. I opened my mouth again to speak, but no words came out. Then, with one last, trepidatious glance at that churning ceiling, I headed for the door.

CHAPTER EIGHT

Dad hadn't been happy. He had been expecting me, an eleven-year-old kid, to be able to sway *that girl.* As if I could convince someone like that to see reason, to see that closing the gate wasn't just doing what *I* wanted. But that leaving it open was probably going to destroy both our lives.

The truth was, though, that nothing else happened for the rest of the week. Aside from Ralph's bobbing head, I didn't see another nasty, and I started to wonder if maybe she *did* have things under control. Maybe she was different from my family. Dad had said she was a medium, that she could open doorways that the rest of us couldn't budge. Did that mean she had some sort of special talent, that she was more powerful than all of us?

The idea irritated me and made me feel jealous at the same time.

But on Friday, everything changed.

I hadn't seen much of Abigail. I only really got a chance to see her once a day. Twice if you counted detention. But on Friday, she seemed shaky when she walked into class, and Ralph was nowhere to be seen. She moved to the back of the room, her favorite place to hide, and sat down, gripping the sides of her desk. Her eyes were wide and her knuckles white from holding the wood so tight.

I shot her a quizzical look, wondering what it was that had changed. Her hair was a mess, a big matt of knots at the side of her head as though she had been in a wrestling match. She saw me looking at her, but as soon as she did her familiar stoic face returned. She turned her body away from me in her seat and focused on Ms. Walker instead.

Between classes, though, I caught her.

"What's going on?" I asked, releasing her arm where I had grabbed it.

Around us, lockers slammed, making her jump.

"What?" she said. "What do you mean?" She looked as guilty as a thief.

I squinted at her.

"Where's Ralph?" I asked.

She looked away, down the hallway towards her next class.

"He, uh, didn't want to come today, I guess." She looked worried.

"What? Since when?" I asked. "I've barely ever seen you without him."

"I, uh—" Her eyes were darting over every surface of the hallway as though she expected it to explode at any moment. "I have to go."

She turned and walked away so fast I didn't have a chance to catch her again. The bell rang and kids scattered, racing towards their next classes before getting caught out of bounds.

But I just stood and stared.

What was going on?

It wasn't until I got home, though, that I really started to worry. Tyler bounded off the bus and ran towards the house. Tyler has an appetite like no kid I've ever met, and his after school hours were usually spent gorging himself on anything our mother would let him eat.

I followed slowly behind, lost in thought, my own

rumbling stomach a distant irritation. I hadn't seen Abigail once for the rest of the day. Not at lunch. Not at break. Not in detention. I felt sure that something was wrong, but at a complete loss about how to get her to admit it.

I walked right through Minnie without even noticing her there, and the shock of the cold sent me yelping to get away.

"Argh!" I said, jumping up and down from foot to foot. I felt frozen, like my blood had in instantly crystallized upon making contact with the ghost. "Oh, hi," I said, realizing what had happened.

Minnie looked horrible. At least as horrible as a ghost can look. She hovered before me, staring at the ground, looking up nervously every few seconds to see if I was still standing there.

"What's up?" I asked.

She opened her mouth, but only a little sigh came out.

Suddenly, I remembered that I had been wanting to talk to Minnie. Or, rather, that she had been wanting to talk to me.

"Is…is there something you want to tell me?" I asked, rubbing my palms over my arms, trying to coerce the blood beneath my skin to start flowing again.

Slowly, she nodded.

I bent over a little bit, trying to catch her eye. She opened her mouth again, and the words that came out were so quiet it seemed like they had been buried within her for a thousand years.

"It's open," she whispered. "The gate."

She knew.

"Yeah, I know," I said.

"He's coming." She rubbed her hands against her arms as if she were as cold as I was.

"Who?" I asked. "Someone is coming?"

She nodded.

"Is it something—someone bad?" I asked.

Her big round eyes looked up into mine, terrified, and I had my answer.

"How do you know?" I breathed.

She shuddered a little.

"I can see," she said, turning to look down the hill, out over the town. Her eyes were trained on the neighborhood where Abigail lived with her family. "And I can feel." She shivered again.

"Wait here," I said, my mind reeling. "I'm going to go get Dad."

She shook her head.

"He needs to hear this," I said. "Just wait."

I turned and ran up the path towards the door, burst through it and flew up the staircase.

"Dad!" I hollered. The attic looked like a bomb had gone off inside. Books lay open, spread out on every surface. A sandwich, maybe lunch, sat forgotten on the big oak desk beneath the window. "Dad!" I called again, hoping to see him stumble out from behind some nook he was studying in.

"Zander!" It was Mom, calling me from the foot of the stairs. I raced to the doorway.

"Mom, where's Dad?"

"I thought he was with you," she said.

"No." I looked around the room again, searching for a clue as to where he had gone. It was then, perched innocently on a bare spot of bookshelf that I saw them.

Dad's glasses.

I lurched towards the bookshelf and grabbed them. Flipping them over in my hands, I saw that one of the lenses was cracked. Why on Earth would he have left these here? The hairs stood up on my skin. I stuffed the glasses into my pocket.

Then I was running again.

"Minnie!" I yelled. I jumped down the front steps of the house, scouring the front yard for the shy little ghost. The sun was beginning to set over the valley, and I could see in the distance that a storm was approaching. "Minnie!" I repeated. I ran all the way around the outside of the house, searching for her. But she had gone into hiding, too frightened by whatever it was that was coming next. Or, maybe, scared by the sound her own voice had made as she had sounded the warning.

My mind was reeling. Dad was gone. Abigail was gone. Minnie had gone underground.

The only one left was me.

I pulled out the glasses and put them on, hoping for a clue. Hoping to somehow, magically, see the location of my father. My protector. My guide.

Instead, what I saw as I looked out over the valley nearly knocked me to the ground. The long, green spectral trails we had been watching for days had now turned blood red. The center of the glow, where all the legs of the beast met, was exploding like a volcano, shooting fire and light up into the darkening sky. My breath caught in my chest as I watched the scene. With each burst of fire that went up, a black, smoky shape came down. As each one hit the center, the whole thing grew bigger and more powerful.

I was frozen in place, caught. Part of me wanted to run back inside and hide under my bed. Like Tyler, I'd just burrow in and hope that the big people could figure out how to fix this.

But my big person wasn't anywhere around. For all I knew, I was the only one seeing this.

So I gulped down my fear, gripped the amulet in my fist, and ran.

Not towards Abigail's house, where we had seen the great spidery trails on previous nights. But towards the place over which it hovered right now, probably right over wherever it was that Abigail was hiding.

Plainsbury Middle School.

CHAPTER NINE

It follows her.

The thought entered my mind all on its own as my feet flew down the ragged sidewalk. I ripped off the glasses and stuffed them in my pocket. I could barely see through them. Watching the burning glow of evil was like looking at the sun on a clear day, and the crack that now ran through the left lens bent the light into a thousand beams, stinging my eyes. I would use them again when I got closer, I told myself. But I knew I wouldn't have to. I knew where I was going, and I had a pretty good idea of what I was going to find when I got there.

As I rounded the corner and dashed towards the school, I was brought up short by something I didn't expect to see.

Kids.

Everywhere, kids. A long line of cars was dropping off students at the school as if it were Monday morning.

But this was different. They weren't in any rush to get inside. Clusters of girls stood whispering and giggling, shooting nervous glances at the few boys who milled around, kicking rocks with their hands stuffed into their pockets. Then I noticed something else that didn't make sense. These girls were all in skirts and dresses. Their hair had been curled or swept up or adorned with sparkling gems. Several, I could see, had painted their eyes and mouths, making them nearly unrecognizable and oddly interesting. The boys looked mostly the same as usual, except that they were all so *clean*. It was as if they had run home after school and allowed their mothers to scrub them raw, their faces unusually pink after the coating of grime had been peeled off. Or maybe their faces were so pink from all of the attention the girls were giving them. And I realized, with a sinking, sickening feeling, what it was I had stumbled into.

The dance.

It was the Fall Harvest Dance I had seen posters for

all over school. I hadn't given it a second thought. I didn't *dance*, for crying out loud. And I had had other, much more serious things to be concerning myself with this week.

With shaking hands I pulled out the glasses and put them on.

Fire. It was like standing in front of an enormous inferno, flames raging as they reached for the sky. And now, I could see, that those weren't just puffs of smoke that were falling back down into the center.

They were nasties.

Pulled into our reality from beyond, swarming into the school like a cloud of angry bees.

I started backing up, my urge to flee overcoming any desire I had to stay and fight. Then, before I had a chance to turn and run, I was on the ground.

I had backed right off the curb.

The loud, angry sound of a car horn blasted in my ears and I looked up to see the towering form of a giant SUV. I gripped the pavement, breathing hard, and hauled myself upright. I stared at the front of the car for a moment, dazed. The father, bald with a scruffy beard, glared at me through the windshield.

"You comin' or goin'?" he yelled out the open

driver's side window.

I stepped back onto the curb, watching him peel out as he navigated his way away from the scene of a hundred sixth graders sizing each other up.

I pulled the glasses off my face.

No need.

I turned to face the entrance to the school.

Just breathe.

And ran.

I shoved my way through the group of girls gathered on the top step, waiting for Ms. Walker to open the doors and announce that the dance had officially begun.

But I didn't wait. I pushed them aside and wrenched open the door, just barely slipping through Ms. Walker's grasping hands as she called out in protest, and ran down the hallway. For a moment I heard her footsteps behind me in pursuit, but then she must have stopped and turned back to the crowd of kids, not wanting to let any more of them slip through.

"Detention, Mr. Casey!" she called after me.

I rounded the corner and started shouting for Abigail. There was no use in sneaking around now. I needed to get to her, fast.

"Abigail!" I yelled, my voice bouncing off the walls,

echoing down the corridor. Above, the ceiling boiled and bucked. It was only a matter of time. "Abigail!" I shouted again.

I opened every classroom door. Shouted into every bathroom. But it wasn't until I reached detention hall that I found her.

"Zander?" a small voice peeped from the shadows.

She was hiding at the far corner of the room, barricaded by a row of desks, shrunken down like a frightened kitten. She looked like she had been hit by a tornado.

"What are you doing in here?" I asked. "They're coming! *He's* coming! We have to stop it!"

Abigail burst into tears.

"I don't know what happened," she cried. "They just all started coming and I couldn't make them stop. I tried to find you, but you'd gone. I'm—I'm cursed, Zander!"

"You're not cursed," I said. I tried to sound supportive, but the truth was that I was a little distracted at the moment. "My dad says you have a gift."

"But it's not a gift," she wailed. "I can't control it. And I keep hearing *him*." She took the base of her hand and banged it against the side of her head.

"Him who?" I asked, shoving one of the desks aside.

"I—" she snuffled, "I think it's the leader. Of the flyers."

"We have to get out of here," I said. "Everyone in the school is about to get attacked.

"What?" she asked. "What do you mean?"

"The dance," I huffed, tossing another desk. "It's tonight. Everyone's here."

Her face froze, horrified.

"Everyone?"

"Pretty much," I said. I grasped for her, but she shrunk farther into the corner.

"Come on, we have to go."

"What are we going to do?" she asked.

"All we can do," I said, holding up the amulet. It twinkled, even in the dim light of the classroom. It must have been able to sense that its time was approaching.

I held out my hand again, and this time she took it.

We raced down the hallway towards the auditorium.

"What is that thing, anyways?" she asked.

"It's a banisher," I said. "When a parallel focuses on a nasty through it, it shoots a jet of power."

"What happens to the…to the nasties?" I noticed she hadn't used the word "flyer".

"I don't know, really," I said, unsure, myself. "It

banishes them, I guess. They always go up in a puff of smoke."

"Does it hurt them?" she asked. She looked worried, not for herself or for everyone else with us in the building, but for the nasties.

"Are you kidding me?" I asked.

Her footsteps echoed mine as we pounded down the hallway.

"I'm just asking," she mumbled.

Argh!

"The truth is, I don't really know," I said. And it *was* true. All I had ever been taught was how to get rid of nasties, not how to keep them safe in the process.

As we rounded the corner into the hallway that led to the dance, both of us stopped in our tracks, our irritation with each other forgotten in an instant.

Here, the mere threat of the nasties above our heads had vanished, replaced with a torrent of the sickening beasts bursting through the ceiling tiles, swimming through midair right through the heavy double doors into the auditorium.

"Oh, no," I breathed.

We crept up to the doors, trying to remain unseen. We were mostly successful. Only one of them caught a glimpse of us, spitting in our direction as he flew away towards more desirable prey.

Into the Harvest Dance.

CHAPTER TEN

The scene was horrific.

And yet I found a nervous laugh escaping my throat.

At least a hundred nasties, in all shapes and sizes, were abusing the patrons of the dance. It seemed that the girls were mostly being targeted, probably because their screams of horror were so shrill, exciting the nasties. Neatly coiffed hairdos were suddenly floating in midair. The little clusters of girls stared at one another, terrified by the ghostly appearance of their friends as their clothing was picked and torn at by hordes of nasties nobody but Abigail and I could see. One of them, a particularly vile and hairy creature, had taken it upon himself to fly around the room, blowing up the skirt of any girl who had dared wear one. Soon the place was echoing with screams as the horrified girls fought to keep their skirts down.

The boys, all clustered off to one side of the gym, stood laughing and pointing at the spectacle.

Until they became the next targets.

Bowls of potato chips, cups of punch, and one entire platter of hummus and vegetables floated their way over the heads of the boys before, *splat*, they were taken out. Suddenly their smiles flipped to surprise and then anger as they realized that they were not immune to whatever joke it was being played.

Now the girls were laughing, and the nasties, too. They bounced up and down on the heads of the boys, smearing the condiments deep into their newly-washed hair, snickering as they teamed up to bonk the boys' heads together. The boys, trying to fight back, punched at empty air in their attempts to stop the onslaught.

But then, suddenly, the mood turned. The nasties got angry, seeming to feed off the outraged swipes of the boys. They started ripping at clothes, shoving people down. Soon the whole room was screaming, and kids were running for the doors.

I held up the amulet and took aim as the last of my classmates shoved their way through the double doors.

The first five nasties evaporated without any of the others being the wiser. But with the sixth, a swarm of them near the doors started to realize their cohorts were vanishing. They turned and, seeing me, started in my direction, their other targets forgotten.

"Uhh…Zander!" shouted Abigail.

I don't know why I did what I did next. It was almost as if my hand had a mind of its own. I felt my fingers rip the amulet from around my neck and thrust it in front of Abigail's face. She looked at the heavy purple stone for a moment, and then, her face changing from frightened to fierce, snatched it and held it up to her eye.

The stone seemed to lock itself into place over her vision, and with one look the entire gang of nasties from the doorway was instantly obliterated, vanishing in an explosion of smoke and dirt.

"Whoa," I said, stunned. "Nice one."

But Abigail wasn't listening. And, I realized, she wasn't even holding the amulet at all.

Her face had changed. Her mouth hung partly open, her eyes stared wide through the crystal stone that hovered now in front of her.

Wherever she looked, nasties exploded. Within sixty seconds, the entire room was empty but for the dust that rained slowly down onto the snack-splattered dance floor.

"Awesome!" I said, clapping her on the back. "I didn't know you could do that! Why didn't you tell me?"

But Abigail wasn't listening.

"No," her mouth formed the word again and again, silent and dazed. "Denied."

Denied?

"Abigail?" I asked. "You okay?"

She was staring straight up at the ceiling, her eyes focusing beyond it, as though she could see right through the wood and beams.

I fumbled for the glasses and smashed them onto my face.

A nasty. No, a *monster*, larger and more terrifying than any nasty I had ever seen or dreamt of, floated above the school. And it was fighting to get inside, pounding its enormous body against a clear barrier between us and him, squeezing its form up against the boundary like a kid smashing his nose against the front window of a candy store.

"No," Abigail breathed again.

The whole building shook as the monster thrust itself against the barrier again and again. It roared at her and I shrunk back, a deep desire flooding through me to hide under one of the few tables that hadn't been overturned.

But Abigail stood tall, not moving an inch.

Slowly, mercilessly, the amulet rose in front of her left eye. She focused, and in the moment before the beast was obliterated, it's face morphed from enraged to shocked.

ZAP!

The barrier dissolved, and the king of the nasties began to fall.

ZAP! ZAP!

It was too big for her to take in one go, but she kept at it, she didn't stop. Finally, with one last, pitiful scream, the entire monster exploded in a gigantic inferno. When the flames disappeared, the monster's remains rained down on us like demonic snowflakes, coating the floor of the gym.

Abigail shook herself a little bit, released from her own power, and turned to me. Slowly, we approached each other, both of us stunned and silent.

And then, Abigail Stone did something I had never seen her do, never expected to ever see her do.

She laughed.

CHAPTER ELEVEN

"I can't believe you did that," I said.

"Neither can I," she said.

"I can," said a voice from behind us.

We swung around and saw Dad. He wore a different set of spectacles over his glasses, these ones newer and more complicated, with filters and buttons. And trailing in his wake with the gait of someone a hundred years old was Gramps.

"Dad!" I yelped, running towards him and practically knocking him down with my hug.

"Amazing!" he said. "Allison—"

"Abigail," I corrected.

"Yes, of course, Abigail. What amazing work! I never would have expected an untrained parallel to handle an alpha. And all on your own!"

"I don't understand," she said. Her giggling faltered, and she looked confused. "What happened, exactly?"

"Wait," I said. "Don't you remember?"

"Kind of," she said. "But some of it seems…"

"Strange?" asked Dad. "Like you were watching it from underwater?"

She turned to him, shocked.

"Yes," she said. "What was that?"

"Well, as we've been trying to tell you, dear, you're a medium," Dad said. He was so excited, bouncing up and down, that I was pretty sure he was the only one who had come close to actually dancing at the Harvest Dance. "When a medium uses an instrument of power, sometimes things can get a little bit murky. But it's always for the best. Mediums are, when the chips are down, always good at heart."

Abigail tilted her head slightly, as if trying to convince herself that she had heard him correctly.

I stifled a snort, but then got control over myself.

"But it was weird, Dad," I said. "It was like she was…possessed or something."

"Not possessed," chimed Gramps, stepping forward. "Locked on."

91

"When Abigail here looked through your amulet," Dad continued, "she alone could see what needed to be done to get rid of the alpha. That's what makes a medium a medium. They know how to access the defensive parts of their souls in a way that's much more powerful than an ordinary parallel."

"And when you got the right tools, and the focus comes, the beasties go *poof!*" said Gramps. He looked, unmistakably, like Tyler right after launching one of his pranks. Then he smiled wide, and this time the snort that had threatened in my throat before came out.

He had forgotten to put in his false teeth today.

I was still giggling as Abigail approached us.

"Well, he helped," she said, nudging me with her elbow.

"Course he did," Gramps said, walking up to the both of us and put one hand on each of our heads, patting us like dogs.

"I found Gramps down in the basement today when I saw what was going on at the school. He dug out his old spectacles for me." Dad fiddled with the dials and knobs on the glasses, impressed by their complexity. "I see you found the others."

"Why didn't you tell me?" I asked. I had been

mighty freaked out without him to tell me what was going on.

"Didn't have time," he said. "Besides, it looks like you did just fine without me."

It was true. My face burned red at the praise, and I was glad that the lights in the gym were low so no one could see.

Then, a sound coming from the doorway made all of us jump. Ralph, cackling and singing, came flying through the air like a bullet towards Abigail. Both Dad and Gramps immediately held up their amulets.

"Wait!" I cried, moving between them and Abigail, where Ralph had stopped, twirling around her head. She laughed. "Don't hurt him! He's her friend."

Dad looked at me like I was insane.

"Her friend?" he asked.

"Yeah, I told you before," I said. "And I know Ralph. He's not so bad. Can't he stay?"

Both Dad and Gramps stared for a moment as Ralph rubbed his slimy body against Abigail's cheek. He seemed relieved that the whole event was over.

I looked back to Dad, silently pleading. Gramps was giving him the same look. Finally, after a long moment, Dad dropped his amulet back to his chest.

"Alright, then," he said. "But just for now, and *only* because the gate is already closed. I'd like to keep it that way for at least a little while. But if he starts to bring more nasties back in, or causes any other trouble..."

"He won't cause any trouble, Mr. Casey," Abigail said, walking towards him. "Ralph, this is Mr. Casey. Mr. Casey, Ralph."

For a fleeting, insane moment I thought that the two might even shake hands at the introduction. Instead, though, Ralph turned around and blew a big fart into Dad's face.

"Ugh!" Dad yelled. And, in fact, we all held our noses and ran from the place, desperate to escape the cloud of stench from the tiny monster.

But I couldn't stop laughing, and as we escaped the trashed auditorium and stumbled into the hallway, everyone cracked up.

"Nice to meet you," Dad said. He wiped tears from his eyes, from the laughing or from the pungent smell, I couldn't tell.

Ralph zoomed around all our heads then, giving us the same sort of special treatment he usually reserved for Abigail. He bounced up and down on the top of my head, careful not to rip into my scalp with the claws on his feet. Then, he leaned over until I saw his face upside down in front of mine. He puckered his slimy lips and planted a big, nasty kiss right on my forehead, like a mom tucking their kid in bed at night. Except gross. And smelly.

But maybe, I thought, I could be friends with a nasty, after all.

Another suspension, this time for two days, and a full two weeks of detention awaited us when all was said and done. It was pretty much impossible to explain to Mr. Fitzsimmons what had happened without giving up our secret, and neither of us wanted anyone to know about what had actually occurred.

Dad was supportive. He explained to Mom all about the battle we had fought without help from him or Gramps, and though it was her tendency to look for whatever it was we were doing that was against the house rules, she was impressed. She even excused our school punishments when Dad told her how I had helped Abigail shut the gate. She kept Abigail, myself and my father up to our eyeballs in cookies and cake for as long as our punishments lasted. Dad, I think, liked this part better than anybody, and it was unusual to see him in the weeks that followed with his face *not* covered in some sort of frosting.

So, as determined by a very anxious and unforgiving Mr. Fitzsimmons, Abigail and I spent every day after school in detention for what seemed like the better part of an eternity. With us was Conrad Smithe, also busted for showing up to the dance with a fake wound in his chest that squirted blood when he pressed a button in his pocket. It might have been funny to the boys, but Veronica Jacobs wasn't too happy when her lavender dress got sprayed with the stuff. It had been assumed that Conrad had been in on the rest of the chaos with me and Abigail, and though we tried to argue at first, eventually we let it drop. Nobody wanted to hear about how one of the biggest trouble makers at school was, in truth, innocent.

Abigail and I, I knew, hadn't learned whatever lesson it was Fitzsimmons was trying to teach us. But we *had* learned a whole lot more. About nasties. About what it meant to be a parallel. And a medium. And about friendship.

We were an unlikely pair, but a month after the Harvest Dance, Abigail's mother finally let her come over to my house. Dad had been trying for weeks to talk to Mrs. Stone, to convince her, somehow, that I wasn't such a horrible kid. And to explain that we would be supervised during her entire visit. *Heavily* supervised.

But it was Mom who finally got Mrs. Stone to give in. She had visited her house with a plate of triple chocolate chip cookies, and had explained that Dad was a little eccentric. He was a scientist, she fibbed, and she told her that sometimes the most brilliant acted the most peculiarly. She also explained that she, however, was a stickler for rules. That she had been mortified by my involvement with what had transpired at the dance. But that she thought that Abigail and I were becoming good friends, and wouldn't it be nice if we could visit each other's houses. Mrs. Stone had confided that Abigail had rarely made friends in any other place, and eventually she relented, agreeing to a visit. As long as Mom was home the entire time.

So, on that crisp fall afternoon, winter already threatening to freeze the tips of our noses, the doorbell rang. I heard Edgar in the hallway as he opened it wide for my very first-ever visitor. I walked up behind him.

"Hi," I said.

"Hi." Abigail grinned. Around her neck dangled a big, intricately cut amulet, red and enticingly dangerous.

97

It had been a gift from my father.

"I can't believe she let you come," I said.

"Yeah." She turned back and waved towards her mother.

At the end of our walk I saw Mrs. Stone's pink minivan, idling silently as she watched us with eyes like a hawk. I smiled and waved in her direction, too. She didn't wave back, but as she pulled away from the house, I could have sworn I saw her crack a smile.

"Well," I said, watching the van dodge the potholes in the road as it glided down the hill. "Come on in."

I swung the door open wide, and Abigail stepped inside.

Mother of two, horse enthusiast, and serial entrepreneur, J. B. Cantwell calls the San Francisco Bay Area home. In her books she explores coming of age in an imperfect world, the effects of greed and violence on all, and the miraculous power that hope can have over the human spirit.

www.jbcantwell.com

Made in the USA
Middletown, DE
21 July 2015